A Child's First Library of Values

The Naughty Mole

A Book about Obedience

A Child's First Library of Values

The Naughty Mole

A young mole ignores the wishes of his parents and sets out on an adventure, but he comes to regret his selfish behavior and learns to be more obedient in the future. *The Naughty Mole* is just one of the international storybooks that make up *A Child's First Library of Values,* a series of delightful stories, beautiful illustrations and universal values.

The Naughty Mole

A Book about Obedience

TIME-LIFE KIDS

4

The cold, snowy days of winter have arrived. But inside the moles' house it is warm and peaceful.

"Let's all have a long sleep until the warm spring comes again," say Mr. and Mrs. Mole.

Everybody in the mole family is tucked up in their beds. Except Ben, that is. Ben doesn't feel even a little bit sleepy.

"It's boring to go to bed. I want to stay up and play."

"Be quiet, Ben. Your noise is keeping us all awake," says his father.

"I'm sorry," says Ben.

Ben goes quietly back to bed, but he has a plan.

As soon as everyone is asleep, Ben packs a small
bag and sneaks out of the house.

"Wowww, it's all white!" he says.

As he sets out on his adventure, Ben leaves deep
footprints in the snow behind him.

"Wheee!"
Ben slides down the hill and slips around in the snow.
He is having so much fun he doesn't even notice the big
snowflakes falling around him.

The crisp new snow is just right for building a snowman. Ben gives his snowman some eyes and adds a mouth.

By the time Ben finishes he feels very cold. He wants to go back to his cozy, warm house. But when he looks back, he sees that the falling snow has covered up his footprints. He can't find his way home.

Ben wanders along miserably even though the snow is no longer falling. He doesn't recognize anything and his home feels a long way away.

Then he sees a young mouse skating lightly across an icy pond.

"Hello! My name's Ben. What's yours?"

"I'm Tess. Do you like my skating?"

"Skating looks fun," says Ben. "I think I'll try it."

He slides carefully onto the ice. Soon he reaches the middle of the pond.

But just as he is about to make a turn the ice under his feet begins to creak and crack…

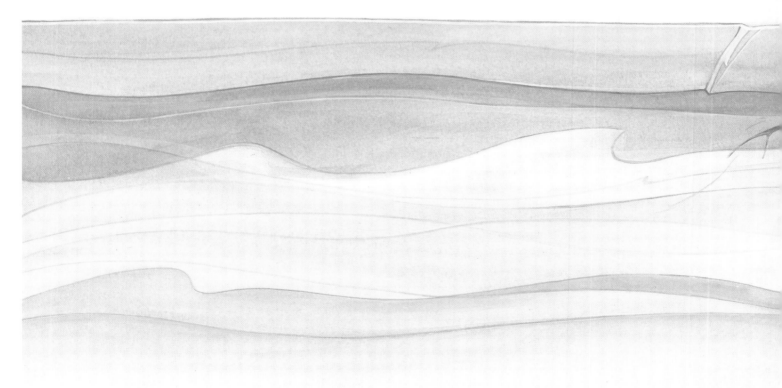

Splash! Ben falls through the hole in
the ice into the freezing water below.
"Help!" cries Ben. "It's so cold."

Luckily, Mr. Rabbit and his son are collecting firewood
nearby. They hear Ben's cry and rush to help him.
"Quick! Catch the rope."

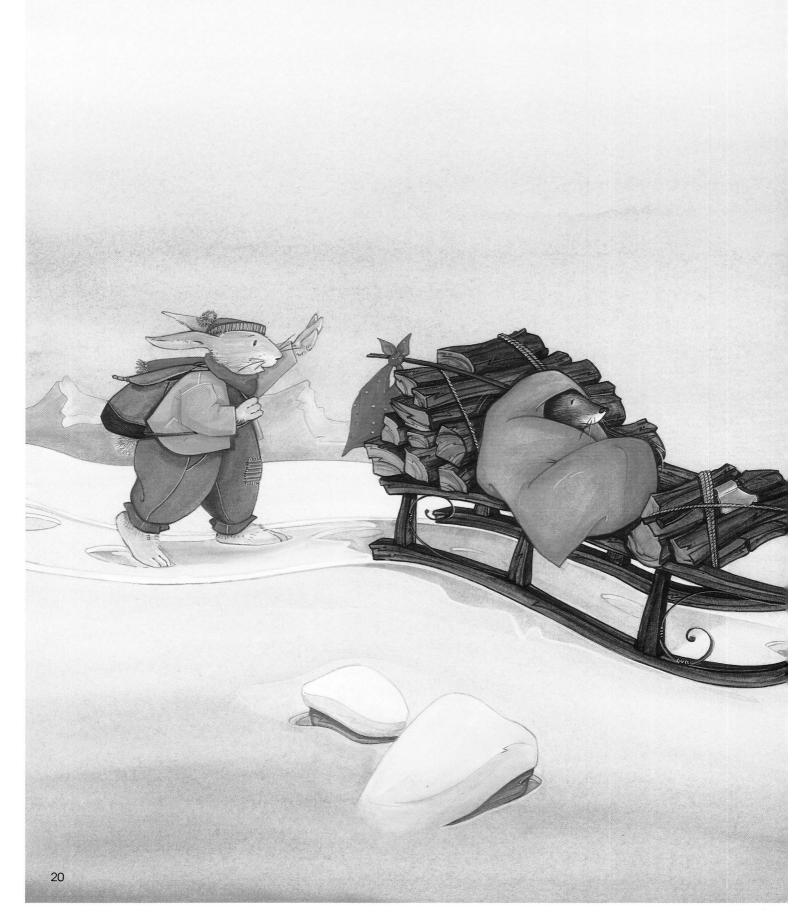

Mr. Rabbit wraps the shivering Ben in a
blanket and lifts him onto their sled.
They set off for the Rabbits' home just as
the sun begins to set.

The Rabbit family hangs Ben's clothes up to dry and leaves him to sleep beside a roaring fire.

"He's so tired," says Mrs. Rabbit. "When he wakes up we will find out where he lives and take him home."

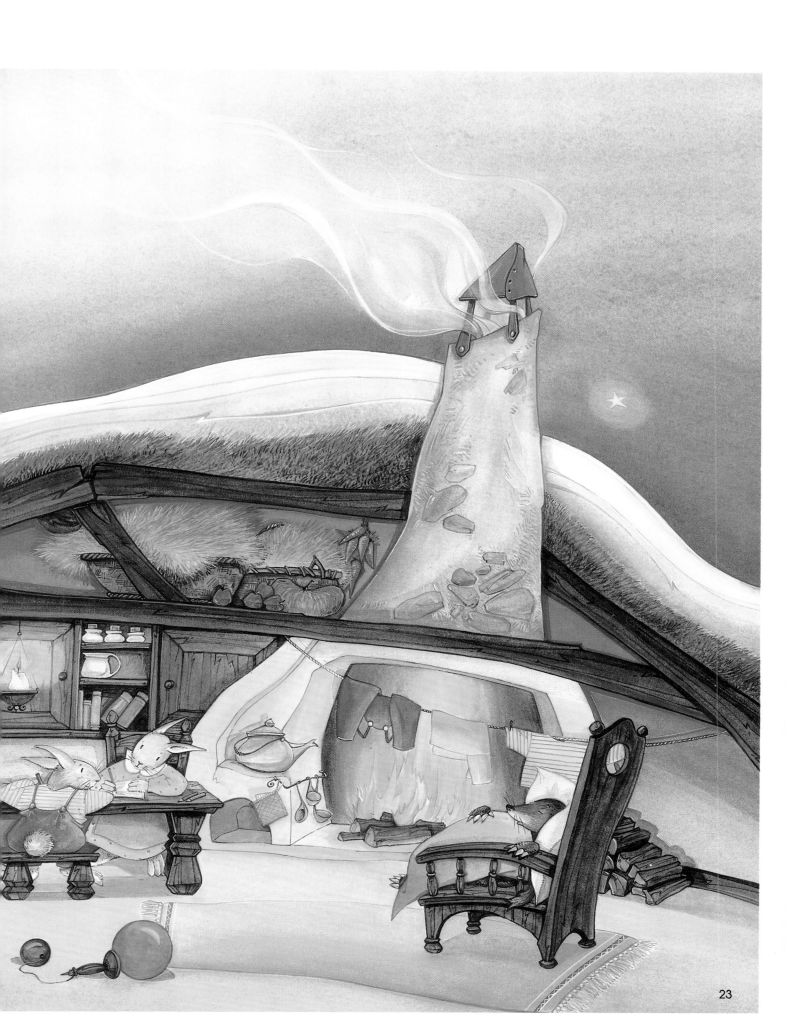

Back at home, Mr. and Mrs. Mole discover that Ben is missing.

"But it's so cold outside," his mother cries.

She lights some lanterns and the whole family
sets off in search of Ben. They are all really worried
about him.

After a while, they come to the house of Mr. Mouse.

"Sorry to disturb you," says Mr. Mole. "We are looking for our son, Ben. We are worried that he is lost in the snow."

"I know where he is," says Tess.

She tells them about skating on the pond and Ben's rescue by Mr. Rabbit.

"Hurry. We must go to the Rabbits' house at once," says Mrs. Mole.

"Ben, thank goodness you are all right," says Mrs. Mole, giving him a big hug. "We were all so worried about you."

The Mole family thanks the Rabbit family for their kindness. Nobody scolds Ben for causing so much trouble.

"I'm sorry I didn't do as I was told, Mommy," says Ben. "I promise never to be so selfish again."

What the story tells us. . .

As parents, we are always seeking ways to reinforce life's important lessons with our children. *A Child's First Library of Values* offers an opportunity for doing so in the context of wonderful, entertaining stories. You may choose to use these books as a springboard for further discussion. The following is a list of universal values reflected in this volume.

- **Going to bed at the right time.** Ben doesn't want to go to sleep at his bedtime, but his parents know how important it is for him to get a full night's sleep—being rested will help him feel better the next day and have the energy to play and do the things he likes to do.

- **Considering the feelings of others.** Ben is making so much noise at bedtime that he keeps his family awake. He is thinking only about himself, and not being considerate of their needs. Young children often have difficulty understanding that everyone else has feelings, too—just like they do. Ben's father reminds Ben of this when he tells him his noise is keeping the rest of the family awake.

- **Obeying parents.** When Ben leaves home without telling his parents, it doesn't occur to him that he might get cold, lose his way, or fall through the ice into freezing water—or even that his absence will cause his parents to worry. Being young, Ben can't realistically judge the dangers posed by the world that exists beyond his sheltered environment. His parents, older and wiser, easily could have predicted all these pitfalls, and worse—that's why they don't allow him to wander off on adventures all by himself.

- **Using good manners.** Saying "sorry," as the Moles do when they disturb the Mouse family late at night, and thanking the Rabbits for their kindness toward Ben shows the Moles' respect and appreciation for others.

- **Telling the truth.** When the Mole family arrives at the Rabbits' house looking for Ben, Tess tells them about his accident and rescue, even though she knows he might get into trouble for running away and for venturing onto thin ice. Not telling the Moles that Ben was safe and sound might have caused his family more worry. Very young children can grasp the fact that people appreciate it when they tell the truth, and as they get older they will also see that people trust them and believe the things they say.

- **Being scolded.** Parents establish rules and set limits because they are responsible for children's safety and well-being. In this story, Ben's parents were so relieved to find him safe at the Rabbits' that they didn't scold him; they could see that he had learned his lesson. Parents correct children's behavior because they love them and know they can do better.

- **Taking responsibility.** When Ben's family comes to get him, he realizes how much trouble he has caused. He apologizes, and promises never to do such a thing again. Ben is developing responsibility and judgment, and realizes that the choices he makes demonstrate to his parents whether he can be considered dependable and trustworthy.

A Child's First Library of Values

The Naughty Mole

Authorized English-language edition published by:
Time Life Asia
VP Time Life International,
*   Regional Director, Asia*
*   and Latin America:*   Trevor E. Lunn
CFO and General Manager: Deepak Desai
Production Manager: Tommy K. Ng
Editorial and New Product
*   Development Manager:*   Kate Nussey
Editor: Vikki Weston
Translation from Chinese: Cathy Poon

First printing 1997. Reprinted 1998.
Printed in Hong Kong.

Time Life Asia is a division of Time Life Inc.

ISBN 0-7835-1300-3

Authorized English-language edition
© 1997 Time Life Inc.

Translated from the Chinese-language edition
© 1995 Time Life Inc.
Original Japanese-language edition published by:
Gakken Co. Ltd., Tokyo, Japan
© 1994 Véronique Bastin/Mikako Shirai and
Gakken Co. Ltd.

Original story and illustration by Véronique
Bastin.
Véronique Bastin was born in Belgium in
1964 and graduated from the Liège School of
Fine Arts. She works in Europe as a writer of
illustrated storybooks.